A NOTE TO PARENTS

Reading Aloud with Your Child
Research shows that reading books aloud is the single most valuable support parents can provide in helping children learn to read.
- Be a ham! The more enthusiasm you display, the more your child will enjoy the book.
- Run your finger underneath the words as you read to signal that the print carries the story.
- Leave time for examining the illustrations more closely; encourage your child to find things in the pictures.
- Invite your youngster to join in whenever there's a repeated phrase in the text.
- Link up events in the book with similar events in your child's life.
- If your child asks a question, stop and answer it. The book can be a means to learning more about your child's thoughts.

Listening to Your Child Read Aloud
The support of your attention and praise is absolutely crucial to your child's continuing efforts to learn to read.
- If your child is learning to read and asks for a word, give it immediately so that the meaning of the story is not interrupted. DO NOT ask your child to sound out the word.
- On the other hand, if your child initiates the act of sounding out, don't intervene.
- If your child is reading along and makes what is called a miscue, listen for the sense of the miscue. If the word "road" is substituted for the word "street," for instance, no meaning is lost. Don't stop the reading for a correction.
- If the miscue makes no sense (for example, "horse" for "house"), ask your child to reread the sentence because you're not sure you understand what's just been read.
- Above all else, enjoy your child's growing command of print and make sure you give lots of praise. *You are your child's first teacher — and the most important one. Praise from you is critical for further risk-taking and learning.*

— Priscilla Lynch
Ph.D., New York University
Educational Consultant

No part of this publication may be reproduced, or stored in a retrieval system, or transmitted in any form or by any means, electronic, mechanical, photocopying, recording, or otherwise, without written permission of the publisher. For information regarding permission, write to Scholastic Inc., Attention: Permissions Department, 555 Broadway, New York, NY 10012.

Text and illustrations copyright © 1997 by Hans Wilhelm, Inc.
All rights reserved. Published by Scholastic Inc.
HELLO READER! and CARTWHEEL BOOKS and associated logos
are trademarks and/or registered trademarks of Scholastic Inc.

Library of Congress Cataloging-in-Publication Data
Wilhelm, Hans, 1945-
　　　Don't cut my hair / by Hans Wilhelm.
　　　　　p.　　cm. — (Hello reader! Level 1)
　　　Summary: A little dog is afraid to get a haircut, but finds that he looks "cool" with short hair.
　　　ISBN 0-590-30700-2
　　　[1. Hair — Fiction. 2. Dogs — Fiction.]　I. Title.　II. Series.
PZ7.W64816D1　　1997
[E] — dc21

96-54486
CIP
AC

19　20

Printed in the U.S.A.　24
First printing, January 1998

DON'T CUT MY HAIR!

by Hans Wilhelm

Hello Reader! — Level 1

SCHOLASTIC INC. Cartwheel B·O·O·K·S®

New York Toronto London Auckland Sydney

I don't want a haircut.

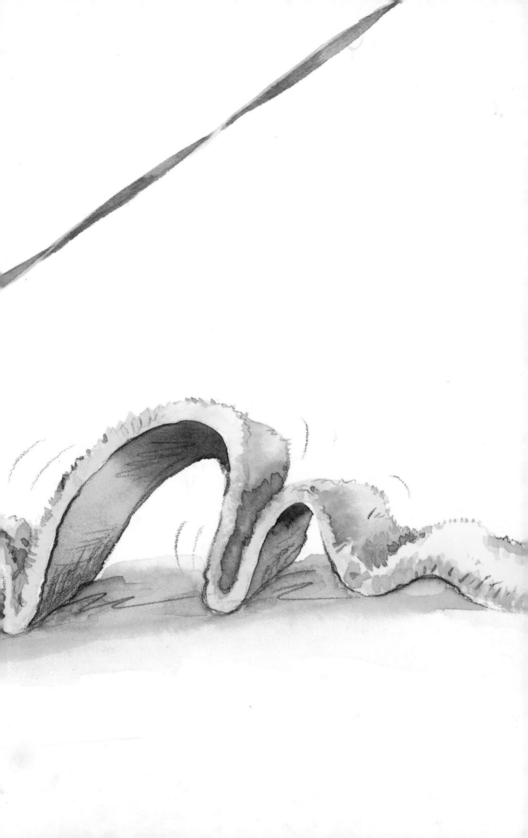

I hate this.

I look silly.

Everyone will laugh at me.

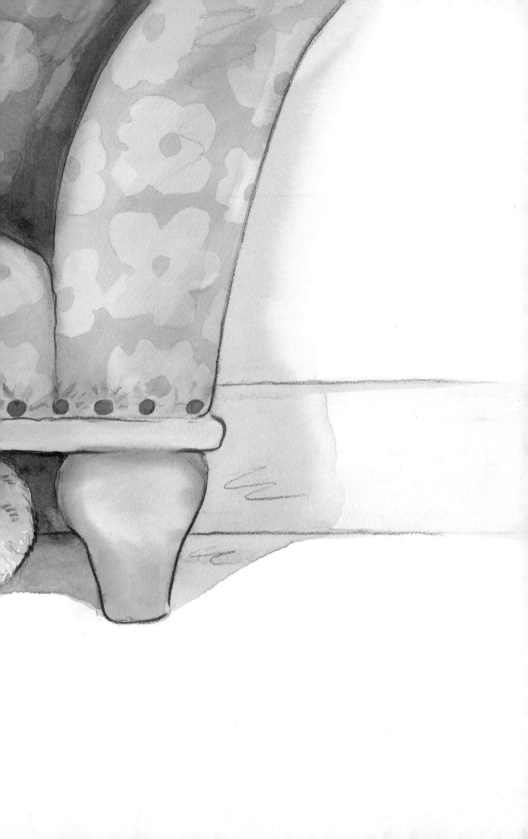

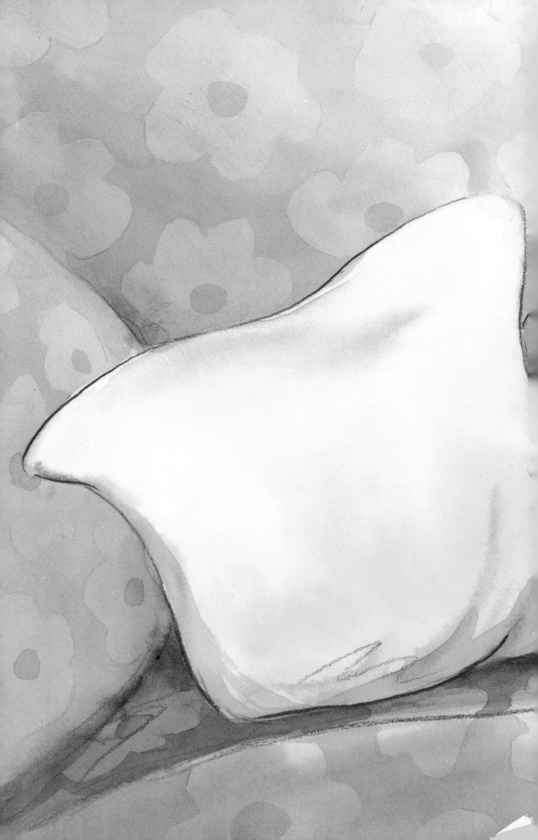

I will never go outside again.

My friends are coming to play.
Oh, no!

They must not see me.

What shall I do?

I have an idea!

Hi, guys. Here I come.

How do you like
my cool new look?

My friends like my cool cut.

They wish they had short hair, too.

I like my new haircut.